world™

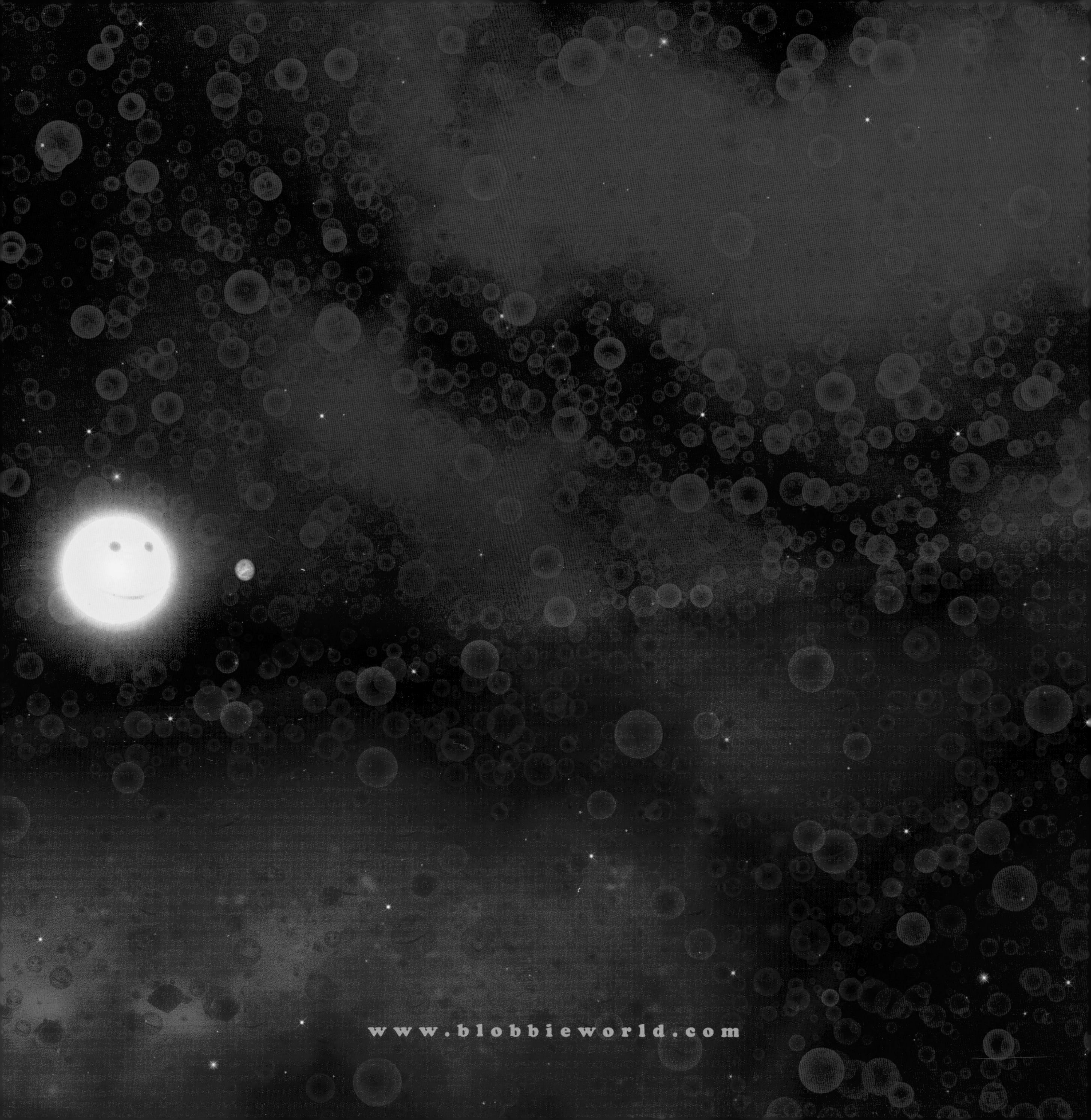
www.blobbieworld.com

Here Come The Blobbies®

written and illustrated by
Jorge Antonio Tello Aliaga
Jorge

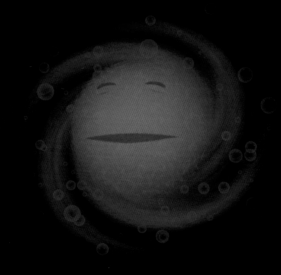

Pers
Publishing
Año 0 : Principio

Publisher's Cataloging-in-Publication
(Provided by Quality Books, Inc.)

Jorge.
Here come the Blobbies / written and illustrated by Jorge.
p. cm.
SUMMARY: Seven colorful young creatures are forced to
escape to a strange planet called Earth, where they must learn
how to use their shape-changing abilities to save the day.
LCCN 2002111938
ISBN 1-932179-32-1

1. Life on other planets--Juvenile fiction.
[1. Extraterrestrial beings--Fiction.]   I. Title.

PZ7.J6872He 2003   [E]
QBI33-1098

Printed in China
First Edition

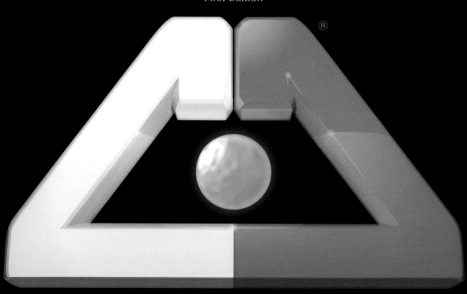

Pers Publishing
5255 Stevens Creek Blvd. # 232-B, Santa Clara, CA 95051

See the Blobbies in action, find out your Blobbie Color personality type and journey through Blobbieworld at:
w w w . p e r s . c o m

Special thanks to:
Dave Valiulis for helping with the editing of this book.
The people at Palace Press International.

This book was put together using Adobe® InDesign® software on a Power Macintosh G4 (while jamming to Madonna's latest hits on iTunes ☺)
The illustrations on this book were created using Adobe® Photoshop® software, Electric Image™ Universe, Strata 3D Pro™, Macromedia® Flash™, and cheap-o™ No. 2 pencils

To my parents:
Sarita y Alberto
**Gracias por ayudarme con los prototipos de los muñecos!
Fue bonito amanecerme con ustedes trabajando** 😊

To my nieces and nephews:
Vanessita, Juancarlitos, Meisita, Valerita,
my yet-to-be-born nephew/niece/godchild 😊,
and Ethancito!
**(Especially Ethancito, since this book was written while I was
in the waiting room — for 2 days! — waiting for Ethancito
to be born, but he would just not come out!
Besides, he LOVES the Blobbies,
or as he prefers to call them:
Babum Babum!)**

Saludos a la tegen de la PUC; Lilianita, Paolita, Lucho, Susy, Abelinho, Vero, Gina, Karim, Eliana, Claudia, Fernando, Kike y Javier · Hi to my blobbie siblings: Evil one, Vinnie, Frederickito, Maricesita, Alikito and Stevecito · Cariños para mi monga y mi chancho (Lilianita y Carlitos), mi cuñadita linda (Meisita) y mi cuñadito feo 😊) (Osquitar) · Paolo + James + Andy: thanks for the help! 😊 · ¡Patticita! 😊 · Tony, don't let me down! 👊 · Hi to my "fans" Grant, Danuele, Nihal, Edsel, Alexander, Cristina and Marcus · Hi Pav! 😊

Somewhere in creation, far far away, there is a world where every grain of sand, every gust of wind and every drop of water can feel, can talk and can smile. This world is known as Blobbieworld ... the home of the blobbies.

Blobbies are peaceful, friendly creatures that can change shape at will. Sometimes they like to be spheres, sometimes they like to be cubes, but no matter what shape they choose, they always wear a smile.

"Arise my children ..." Blobbie Fire extended a limb, and a bright white light burst from it. When the light dispersed, seven round little creatures appeared in space.

As the sleepy newborn blobbies floated by, Blobbie Fire named them after the colors of the rainbow:

Blobbie Red
The Warrior

Blobbie Orange
The Venturer

Blobbie Yellow
The Savant

Blobbie Green
The Healer

Blobbie Blue
The Herald

Blobbie Indigo
The Artisan

Blobbie Violet
The Sorcerer

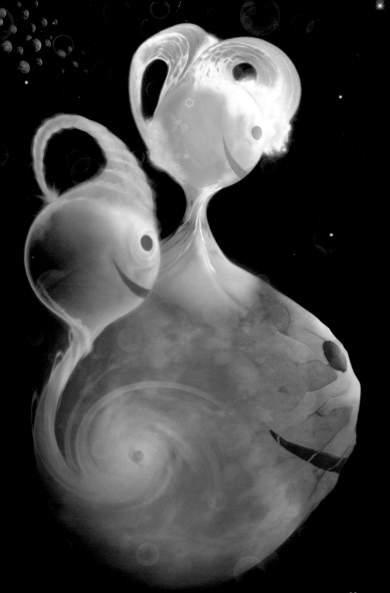

"Welcome, Blobbie Colors," said Blobbie Earth with the voice of crushing rocks, "We are the Blobbie Elements, we are your family."

"We live in space and all around you," said Blobbie Water with the voice of splashing waves, "We are here to protect and teach you."

"Learn, play, be kind and happy ..." said Blobbie Air with the voice of soothing winds, "this is all we ask from you."

"You must now go to Blobbieworld," said Blobbie Fire with the voice of crackling flames, "You cannot stay with us in space. Here sleeps our eldest, Blobbie Void, who should never be awakened."

The seven Blobbie Colors spent their first months of life playing with other blobbies and learning how to blobbiemorph into all the shapes that could be found across Blobbieworld: triangles, hexagons, cones, pyramids, cubes, octahedrons and others.

Blobbie Violet thought it was boring that everything in Blobbieworld was shaped as a sphere or a cube or some other simple shape. "I want to travel into space," it sighed.

"You can't go there," scolded Blobbie Indigo. "Blobbie Void sleeps there."

"But ... can you imagine all the incredible things that must be out there?" said Blobbie Violet looking at the heavens. "And if Blobbie Void is really as old as we've been told ... can you imagine all the things it must know?"

Blobbie Indigo widened its eyes, "Do you think it could teach us new shapes?"

"I'm sure!" Blobbie Violet nodded, "But how could we go into space unnoticed?"

"I think I know a way!" Blobbie Indigo shouted with excitement.

"Blobbiemorph!" said Blobbie Indigo, while it concentrated hard and blobbiemorphed into a perfect copy of an asteroid. Blobbie Indigo then made its body hollow, so that Blobbie Violet could hide inside, and together they left Blobbieworld unnoticed.

The two siblings talked and laughed until they found themselves in front of the enormous Blobbie Void.
Blobbie Violet took a deep long breath and stretched a limb to touch it,
"Wake up, Blobbie Void!"

"Nooooooo!!!" Blobbie Void screamed with the voice of whispering ghosts, as its body expanded and filled with light.

Blobbie Indigo and Blobbie Violet moved back in fear as Blobbie Void's body transformed into a magical doorway from which an army of dark creatures began to emerge.

"The Hexacones have escaped" shouted Blobbie Fire as it found itself surrounded.
"You belong to us!" said the largest Hexacone in a deep monotone voice, as the other Hexacones began blowing winds of cold darkness towards Blobbie Fire.

The Blobbie Elements watched helplessly as their sibling fell asleep, frozen in darkness.

The Hexacones then proceeded towards Blobbieworld and continued their attack.

Blobbie Indigo, Blobbie Violet and the rest of the Blobbie Colors, found themselves in the middle of a full-scale war.

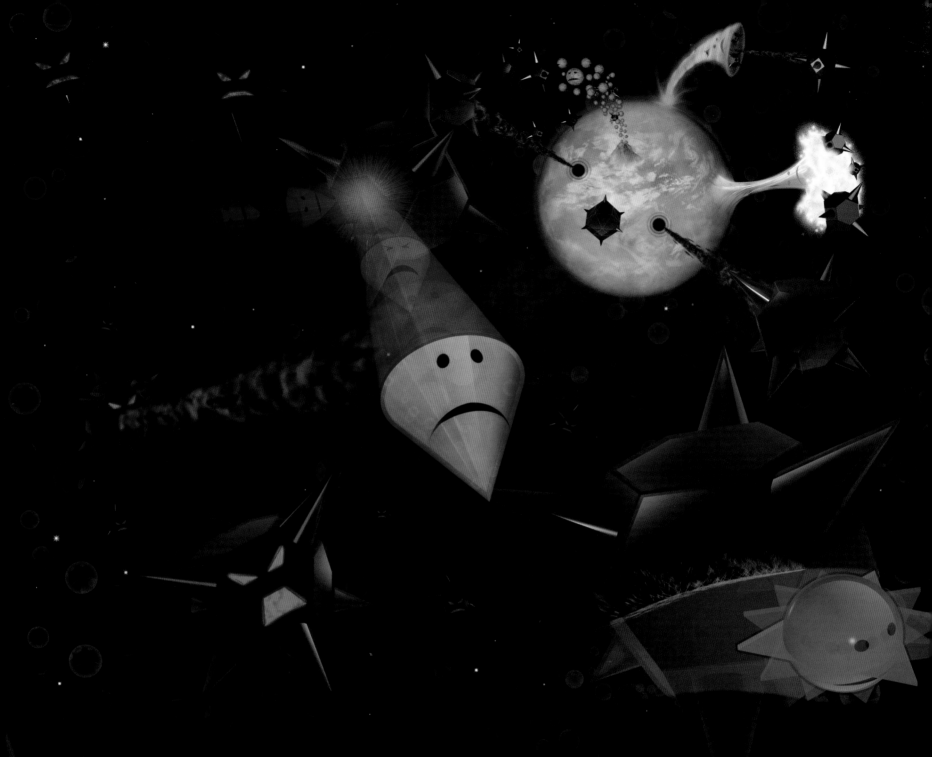

"Blobbiemorph!" yelled Blobbie Red with confidence, as it blobbiemorphed into a strong pointy cone and darted towards one of the Hexacones.

"Blobbiemorph!" yelled Blobbie Violet as it blobbiemorphed into the most powerful shape it could imagine: a rotating trianglesphere.

The young blobbies bravely tried to stop the invaders, but they were easily brushed aside.

"I must save the children!" said Blobbie Void with desperation. "I must take them somewhere safe."

Blobbie Void opened its mouth and sucked all of the Blobbie Colors in. Its body expanded and filled with light, and in the blink of an eye, the blobbie children were transported elsewhere.

"**What happened!?**" Blobbie Yellow asked curiously.

"I have brought you to Planet Earth ... a long forgotten world," answered Blobbie Void. "I kept the Hexacones locked within me for two thousand years, but now they are free and they won't rest until they have enslaved our world. You will be safe here ... but I must return to Blobbieworld."

"**It's all my fault!**" cried Blobbie Violet. "**I should have listened.**"

"**We just wanted to have fun ...**" said Blobbie Indigo with tears in its eyes.

"Don't cry, my children," Blobbie Void slowly faded away. "Take care of each other ..."

"**What do we do now?**" asked Blobbie Red.

"**We explore Earth!**" answered Blobbie Orange.

The blobbies could feel their bodies get heavier and change as they softly fell to Earth.
"Look! Shapes everywhere! Millions of them!" yelled Blobbie Indigo as it
discovered all sorts of rocks, trees and creatures covering Earth. **"Aren't they beautiful?"**
"Way cool!" said Blobbie Orange enthusiastically. **"A whole new world to explore!"**
"With lots of cute little creatures," added Blobbie Green caringly.
"And many things to learn!" shouted Blobbie Yellow with joy.

"I'm going to talk to the creatures of this world!" decided Blobbie Blue as it approached a furry four-legged creature.

Blobbie Blue talked and talked, but for some reason, the four-legged creature did not talk back.

Blobbie Blue then saw a two-legged creature approaching. This creature was tall and had all sorts of clothing covering its skin.

Blobbie Blue ran towards it and started talking to it. The two-legged creature jumped back, and shrieked in some incomprehensible language as it ran away.

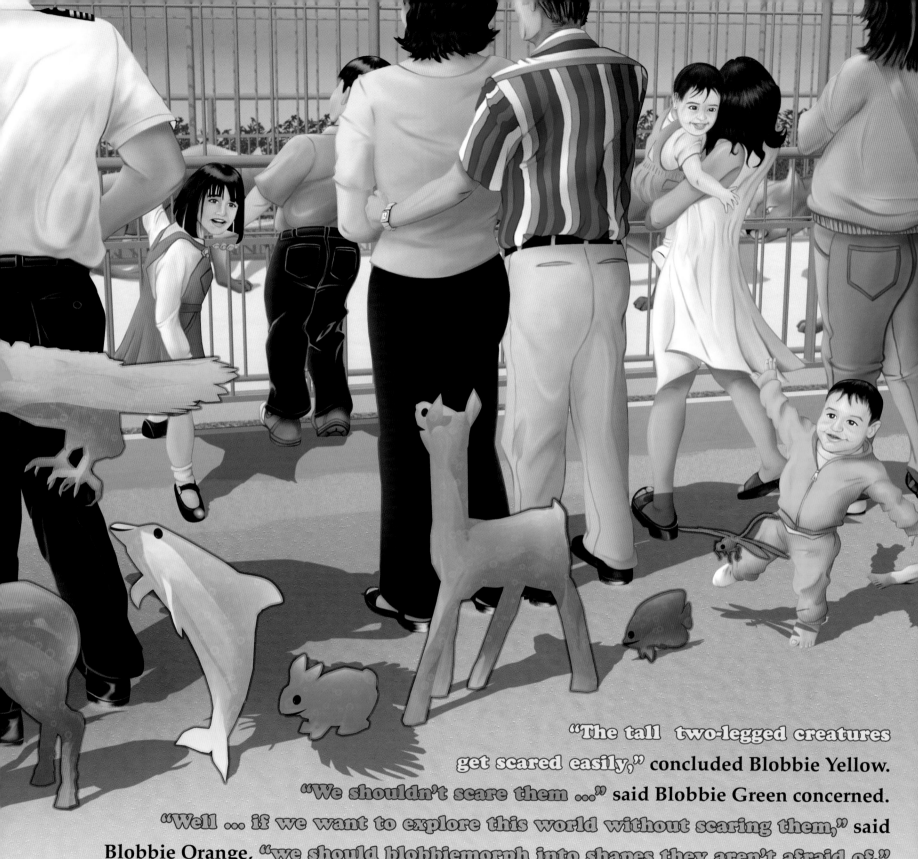

"The tall two-legged creatures get scared easily," concluded Blobbie Yellow.
"We shouldn't scare them ..." said Blobbie Green concerned.
"Well ... if we want to explore this world without scaring them," said
Blobbie Orange, "we should blobbiemorph into shapes they aren't afraid of."
The blobbies agreed and blobbiemorphed into all sorts of Earth creatures.

The blobbies discovered several structures all around them. They entered all of them, one by one, and found new and interesting things.

Blobbie Yellow wandered on its own into other buildings. **"Wow!"** said Blobbie Yellow, as it entered a huge room filled with thousands of books–books that had pictures of incredible shapes in all colors and sizes. **"Hey everyone, look what I've found!"**

For days, weeks, and months, the blobbies studied the books and learned the alien language in which they were written. They learned about Earth and the people of Earth. They discovered new shapes, and learned how to blobbiemorph into them.

Blobbie Violet opened an astronomy book and sighed while remembering Blobbieworld and the trouble its disobedience had caused. Then its face lit up with hope, "We have to go back! With these new shapes we have learned, we should be strong enough to defeat the Hexacones and save Blobbieworld!"

"Let's do it!" shouted Blobbie Red, eager to fight off the invaders.

"Yeah!" agreed Blobbie Orange, "Let's go home!"

"Blobbiemorph!" yelled Blobbie Red as it blobbiemorphed into a huge spaceship.

The other blobbies climbed aboard Blobbie Red and departed Earth. Blobbie Blue then blobbiemorphed into a powerful transmitter and sent a message into space:

"Blobbie Void, where are you? WE NEED YOU! YOU! YOU!YOU!YOU!OU!

"I am here, children," responded Blobbie Void as it came into view.

"We have to go back to Blobbieworld," said Blobbie Orange.

"No!" refused Blobbie Void. "The Hexacones would capture you."

"They won't!" said Blobbie Violet sure of itself. "We've learned powerful new shapes on Earth and we'll find a way to defeat them ... but we need your help."

Blobbie Void hesitated for what seemed like an eternity ... then its body expanded and filled with light, and in the blink of an eye, the blobbies were back home.

The Blobbie Colors were horrified upon looking at their world.

What once was a world full of colors and sounds was now a dark and quiet world … and an army of Hexacones menacingly hovered over it.

"Blobbiemorph!" Blobbie Blue blobbiemorphed into a giant antenna dish. "I can hear them talking! The big Hexacone is giving orders to the small ones."

"That is the Hexacone King," said Blobbie Void. "It is preparing its armies to attack other worlds ... I am afraid they will use me as their transport."

"**Blobbiemorph!**" Blobbie Yellow blobbiemorphed into a scanning telescope, and searched for weaknesses in their attackers.

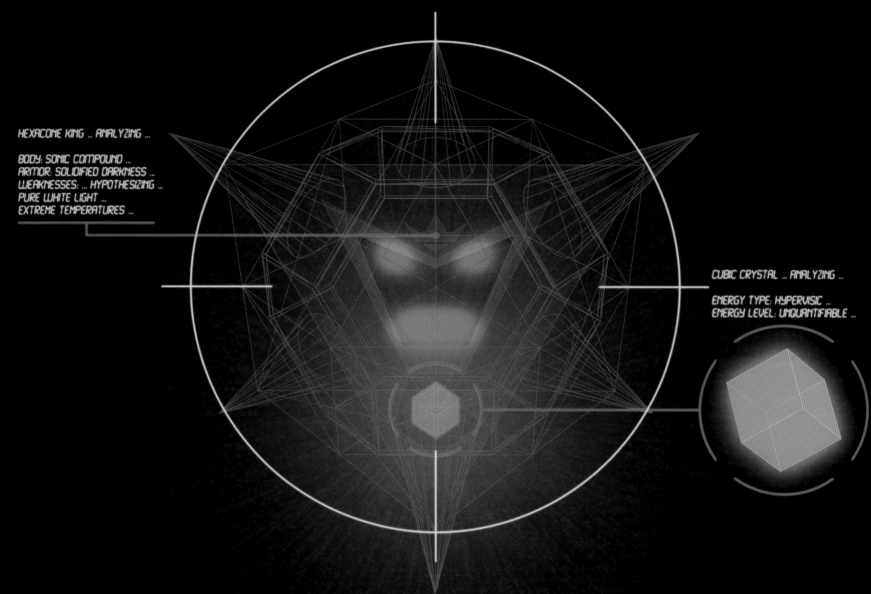

HEXACONE KING ... ANALYZING ...

BODY: SONIC COMPOUND ...
ARMOR: SOLIDIFIED DARKNESS ...
WEAKNESSES: ... HYPOTHESIZING ...
PURE WHITE LIGHT ...
EXTREME TEMPERATURES ...

CUBIC CRYSTAL ... ANALYZING ...

ENERGY TYPE: HYPERVISIC ...
ENERGY LEVEL: UNQUANTIFIABLE ...

"Hmmm ... the Hexacone King is hiding something within its armor," said Blobbie Yellow. "Some sort of cubic crystal ... there is an incredible amount of energy coming from it."

"It's the Hexahedron Crystal!" said Blobbie Void.

"What's that?" asked Blobbie Yellow.

"A legendary source of evil power," answered Blobbie Void, "The Hexacones must be using its power ... that's why they are so strong."

"So ... if we destroy the crystal," concluded Blobbie Yellow, "we might be able to defeat the Hexacones!"

"But how could we approach the Hexacone King?" wondered Blobbie Orange, "It is surrounded by its army!"

"I think I know a way!" Blobbie Indigo shouted with excitement.

Before Blobbie Indigo could share its idea with its siblings, a Hexacone soldier snuck up behind them and blasted winds of cold darkness upon them.

"BLOBBIEMOOOOOOOORPH!!!!!!!!" yelled Blobbie Green in desperation as it blobbiemorphed into a gigantic venus flytrap and tried to protect its siblings by swallowing the blast!

When the dark winds dissipated, Blobbie Green stood frozen in darkness … but the rest of the Blobbie Colors had mysteriously disappeared.

"Where did the children go!?" asked the Hexacone soldier who had attacked the Blobbie Colors.

The colossal Hexacone King flew towards Blobbie Void, followed by its army, "Have you hidden the children from me again?" it asked. "Tell me where they are!"

"NO," Blobbie Void responded firmly.

The enraged Hexacone King turned to the Hexacone soldier on its left and commanded, "MAKE THIS OLD BLOBBIE TALK!!!"

"Blobbiemorph!" replied the Hexacone soldier as its body changed revealing its true identity: Blobbie Indigo in disguise!

The other Blobbie Colors burst from inside Blobbie Indigo's body and followed Blobbie Orange as it lunged towards the Hexacone King in the shape of a swift wild tiger, "This is our chance to destroy the crystal! Everyone, BLOBBIEMORPH!!!"

Blobbie Red blobbiemorphed into a powerful jet fighter and eagerly sprang into action.

Blobbie Yellow blobbiemorphed into a mighty mechanical excavator and calmly entered the battle.

Blobbie Blue blobbiemorphed into a sleek space satellite and faithfully stood by its siblings.

Blobbie Indigo blobbiemorphed into a majestic giant statue and hesitantly joined the fight.

"Enough of this child's play!" The Hexacone King blew winds of cold darkness at the Blobbie Colors.

"Blobbiemorph!" yelled Blobbie Violet as it blobbiemorphed into the most powerful shape it could imagine: a fire breathing batsnake.

Blobbie Violet hit the Hexacone King's armor with flames of light until it shattered, releasing the Hexahedron Crystal.

Energía Fotónica

Blobbie Violet swooped towards the Hexahedron Crystal and used its powerful jaws to crush it into a million pieces.

At that moment, the Hexacone King and its army shrieked as their bodies began to shrink and change.

The Hexacones were blobbiemorphing!!!

The Hexacones had been blobbies transformed into evil creatures by the power of the Hexahedron Crystal. With the crystal destroyed, the Hexacones reverted back to normal, and all the frozen blobbies woke up from their deep sleep.

"Blobbie Green, you are back to normal!" Blobbie Blue hugged its sibling as the rest of the Blobbie Colors thanked Blobbie Green for protecting them.

"Thank you, Blobbie Colors," chimed the blobbie who used to be the Hexacone King, "You've saved us!"

Blobbie Void smiled, "Well done, children!"

"Let's celebrate!!!" cheered Blobbie Orange.

Blobbie Violet, still feeling guilty for what had happened, left the celebration and approached Blobbie Fire, "I'm the one who woke up Blobbie Void, I am sorry ..."

"We told you not to awaken Blobbie Void," Blobbie Fire said disapprovingly. "We almost lost our world ... learn from this experience and grow wiser."

Blobbie Fire smiled kindly, "How did you learn all those new shapes?"

"We learned them on a planet called Earth!" answered Blobbie Violet.

"Planet Earth?" said Blobbie Fire, "I haven't heard of that world in a very long time."

"Can we go there again?" asked Blobbie Violet, full of hope.

Blobbie Fire hesitated for a moment, "Maybe ..."

Pero, ¿y quién creó el Crystal Hexaedro? ...

The many shapes

Favorite Planar Shapes

by revolving on its axis, it blobbiemorphs into ...

Favorite Solid Shapes

Circle
A round planar shape.
Its boundary line is known as
its Circumference.

Sphere
A totally round solid shape.
The most simple and perfect of
all shapes.
The blobbie's favorite shape.

Ellipse
A shape similar to the Circle
but not perfectly round.
An Oval is an imperfect Ellipse.

Spheroid
A shape similar to the Sphere,
but not perfectly round.
Also known as the Ellipsoid.

Rectangle
A four–sided planarshape with
four right angles.
If all its sides have the same
length then it is called a Square.

Cylinder
A solid shape in which its two
sides are circles.

Triangle
A three–sided planar shape.
Also known as the Trigon.

Cone
A Pyramid with a circular base.

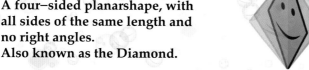

Rhombus
A four–sided planarshape, with
all sides of the same length and
no right angles.
Also known as the Diamond.

Bicone
A shape formed by placing two
cones base to base.
Also knows as the Dicone.

Semicircle
A planar shape creating by
cutting a Circle in half.

Hemisphere
A solid shape creating by
cutting a Sphere in half.

Trapezoid
A four sided planar shape, with
2 parallel sides. Known in some
places as the Trapezium.

Frustum
The shape you get by cutting off
the top of a Cone or any other
type of Pyramid.

# of Blobbieworld™

The Blobbie's Favorite Polygons

Polygons are **closed planar shapes** that have 3 or more sides.
Regular Polygons are Polygons that have all their sides equal in length and all the angles between their sides are also equal.
The first 7 Regular Polygons are:

Equilateral Triangle
A Regular Polygon
with **3 sides** and 3 angles.
A type of Trigon.

Square
A Regular Polygon
with **4 sides** and 4 angles.
A type of Tetragon.

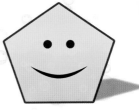

Pentagon
A Regular Polygon
with **5 sides** and 5 angles.

Hexagon
A Regular Polygon
with **6 sides** and 6 angles.

Heptagon
A Regular Polygon
with **7 sides** and 7 angles.

Octagon
A Regular Polygon
with **8 sides** and 8 angles.

Nonagon
A Regular Polygon
with **9 sides** and 9 angles.

The Blobbie's Favorite Polyhedrons

Polyhedrons are **solid shapes whose sides are Polygons.**
Regular Polyhedrons are Polyhedrons whose sides are identical Regular Polygons.
Regular Polyhedrons are known on Earth as **"The Platonic Solids"**, in honor to the greek philosopher **Plato** who wrote about these shapes.
There are **ONLY five Regular Polyhedrons** and they are very important and powerful blobbie shapes:

Hexahedron
A Regular Polyhedron with
6 Square faces,
8 vertices, and 12 edges.
Also known as the Cube.

Icosahedron
A Regular Polyhedron with
20 Equilateral Triangle faces,
12 vertices, and 30 edges.

Octahedron
A Regular Polyhedron with
8 Equilateral Triangle faces,
6 vertices, and 12 edges.

Tetrahedron
A Regular Polyhedron with
4 Equilateral Triangle faces,
4 vertices, and 6 edges.
The Tetrahedron is a Pyramid.

Dodecahedron
A Regular Polyhedron with
12 Pentagon faces,
20 vertices, and 30 edges.

Blobbie Red The Warrior™

Athletic, Energetic, Passionate, Self-Loving, Spontaneous, Instinctive and Courageous.

Blobbie Red loves action and can never sit still. Enjoys doing sports and all kinds of physical work.
Always persistent until reaching its goals. Prefers working and playing in a group rather than alone.
Likes finding challenges. Sometimes a bit selfish and too impulsive.

Blobbie Orange The Venturer™

Adventurous, Enthusiastic, Emotional, Strong-Minded, Outgoing, Leading and Confident.

Blobbie Orange loves nature in all its forms. Enjoys being outdoors, exploring the world and playing with animals.
Always extroverted, sociable and friendly. Prefers being a leader rather than a follower.
Likes to express its emotions. Sometimes a bit inflexible and too opinionated.

Blobbie Yellow The Savant™

Intellectual, Curious, Logical, Practical, Easy-Going, Joyful and Mature.

Blobbie Yellow loves learning and asking questions. Enjoys having fun with its knowledge and building things.
Always responsible and dedicated. Prefers getting along with everybody rather than arguing.
Likes its privacy. Sometimes a bit insensitive and too serious.

Blobbie Green The Healer™

Helpful, Caring, Objective, Understanding, Harmonious, Generous and Humble.

Blobbie Green loves helping others and taking care of everyone. Enjoys growing plants and raising animals.
Always understanding and a good listener. Prefers to live life unnoticed rather than being famous.
Likes to be open. Sometimes a bit needy and too selfless.

Blobbie Blue The Herald™

Communicative, Wise, Serene, Loving, Loyal, Sentimental and Introspective.

Blobbie Blue loves to share its experience and its feelings. Enjoys talking to new people and giving advice.
Always truthful and honest. Prefers having a few close friendships rather than lots of friends.
Likes its independence. Sometimes a bit melancholic and too lonesome.

Blobbie Indigo The Artisan™

Artistic, Creative, Pleasant, Affectionate, Fun, Perceptive and Unconventional.

Blobbie Indigo loves being creative and making beautiful things. Enjoys finding beauty in everything and everyone.
Always good-natured and fun to be around. Prefers looking good and dressing up rather than looking plain.
Likes being different. Sometimes a bit insecure and too sensitive.

Blobbie Violet The Sorcerer™

Imaginative, Inventive, Spiritual, Benevolent, Self-Reliant, Intuitive and Dreamful.

Blobbie Violet loves being a visionary and dreaming up things. Enjoys finding mysterious and magical things in life.
Always striving to be better and improve the world. Prefers creating rather than copying.
Likes inspiring others. Sometimes a bit immature and too prideful.

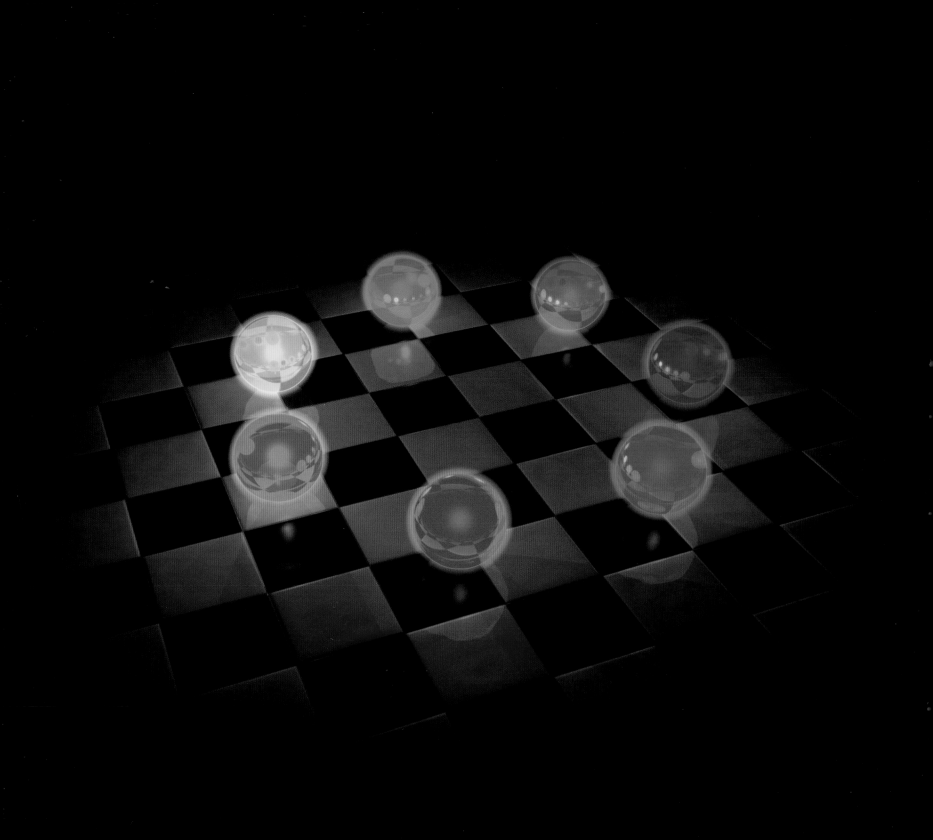

www.blobbieworld.com

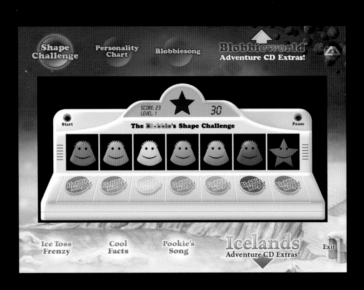

WHICH SHAPE WILL THEY BLOBBIEMORPH INTO NEXT!?
Are you up to the challenge?

FREE Blobbieworld Adventure CD inside.
Featuring: The Blobbie's Shape Challenge
and fun CD Extras such as draft animations and an interactive
Blobbie Personality Chart!
Includes fun songs for your music CD player.
Bonus: Icelands Adventure (starring Pookie and Tushka!)

CD-ROM System Requirements:
Windows®
• Pentium™-class processor (Pentium II or higher recommended)
• Windows 95 or later
• 32 MB or more of installed RAM
• 16x CD-ROM drive or faster
• 800x600 minimum screen resolution

Macintosh®
• Power Macintosh Power PC processor (G3 or higher recommended)
• Mac OS 8.6 to Mac OS X
• 32 MB or more of installed RAM
• 16x CD-ROM drive or faster
• 800x600 minimum screen resolution